Princess Candytuft

For Ruby Brooks
J.W.

For Lily
P.D.

ORCHARD BOOKS
338 Euston Road, London NW1 3BH
Orchard Books Australia
Level 17/207 Kent Street, Sydney, NSW 2000

First published by Orchard Books in 2007

A CIP catalogue record for this book is available from the British Library.

ISBN 978 1 84362 263 5

1 3 5 7 9 10 8 6 4 2

Printed in Singapore

Orchard Books is a division of Hachette Children's Books, an Hachette Livre UK company.

The Secret Fairy®
Princess Candytuft
Jeanne Willis
Penny Dann

ORCHARD BOOKS

It was a very happy day in Secret Fairyland.
A baby had just been born.

It was a very special baby –
a royal baby!

The Tricksy Pixies were the first to know.
They couldn't wait to spread the news.

They climbed onto Snapdragon
and flew to Blossom's house.
'Something brilliant has happened!' they said.

'Let me guess,' said Blossom.
'Have you been good pixies?'

'Oh no, it's much more brilliant than that!' said Teasel.
'A squillion times brillianter!' said Tansy.

'The Fairy Queen has
had a baby!' said Tansy.

The fairies danced up and down with joy.
'Is it a boy or a girl?' asked Blossom.

'It's a boy,' sniggered Teasel.
'He's called Prince Cauliflower,'
giggled Tansy.

'Cauliflower? How charming!' said Hollyhock.
'How modern!' said Bluebell.

'How . . . unusual,' thought Blossom.
'I like cauliflower,' said Fuzzy Caterpillar, 'but I prefer lettuce.'

'The Fairy Queen has invited you to meet him tomorrow,' tittered Tansy. 'You have to bring gifts fit for a prince,' snorted Teasel.

'We know that. We're not silly!' said Nettle. 'Oh yes, you are!' whispered the Tricksy Pixies. But nobody heard.

Each Secret Fairy had to think of a perfect gift to give Prince Cauliflower.

Blossom decided to make him a fluffy crown.
'What colour?' asked Lavender.
'Oh, it has to be blue for a boy,' insisted Blossom.

'Shall I knit him a knight?' asked Bluebell.
'Boys like knights . . . don't they?'
'Of course they do!' said Nettle.

Nettle wanted to make
Prince Cauliflower a drum.
Lavender would make him a football and
Hollyhock would mix him three wish potions,
to make him brave, bold and fearless!

Blossom collected bluebird feathers
to make the crown.
Bluebell fetched some spider's silk
to knit the knight with.

Hollyhock mixed fairy dust,
dew and dragon's tears
to make her wish potions.

Nettle found a nutshell to
make the drum and Lavender
gathered leaves for the football.

They were busy in the
Fairy Workshop all night.
'Oh dear,' groaned Lavender.
'I'll never finish this by morning.'
'Me neither!' wailed Bluebell.

But by midnight, the gifts were ready.
'Bedtime for fairies,' yawned Blossom.

The next day, the fairies took their gifts to the palace. They arrived at the same time as the Tricksy Pixies.

The palace guards led them to the nursery, which was all decorated in . . .

. . . PINK!

'Allow me to introduce Princess Candytuft!' said the Fairy Queen.
'Princess?' gasped Blossom. 'But we were told the baby was a prince!'

'Whoever gave you that idea?'
said the Fairy Queen.
'We don't know, do we, Tansy?'
giggled Teasel.

The Tricksy Pixies gave the baby a frilly dress.
'It's pink for a girl!' grinned Tansy.

'Whatever shall we do?' whispered Bluebell.
'Our gifts aren't fit for a princess!'

'It's the thought that counts,' said Blossom, and she gave the baby her crown.

To her surprise, the Fairy Queen clapped her hands with delight. 'Hurrah, it's blue! My favourite colour.'

Nettle felt anxious as she gave
the baby her drum.
'You can't give a girl a drum!'
hooted Tansy.

'Yes, you can!' said the Fairy Queen.
'I always wanted a drum when I was little!'

Even so, Bluebell was worried about the knight. She offered to make a pretty doll instead. But the Fairy Queen wouldn't hear of it.

'Princess Candytuft is drowning in dolls. She'll adore your knight – he's gorgeous!'

'I've brought her a football, but I could swap it for a necklace,' said Lavender.

'What fun!' said the Fairy Queen. 'Every girl should have a football!'

'What is your gift, Hollyhock?' smiled the Fairy Queen.
Hollyhock didn't like to say, so Blossom held her hand to make her feel better.

'I . . . um . . . I've made her three wish potions,' she said.

'Are they for the Princess to be beautiful, rich and to marry a prince?' asked the Fairy Queen, stifling a little yawn.

'Not quite,' said Hollyhock.
'I wished she would be . . .

brave . . .

bold . . .

and fearless.'

'Fantastic!' said the Fairy Queen.
'That's exactly what I want for my girl!'

The Fairy Queen couldn't thank the fairies enough for their perfect presents.

They kissed Princess Candytuft goodbye and left her cuddling her knight, kicking her football and beating her drum bravely, boldly and fearlessly in her blue crown.

'Princess Candytuft loved our gifts,' said Blossom. 'Even though the pixies tricked us into thinking she was a prince.'

'Maybe they don't know the difference between boys and girls,' laughed Nettle.

'Oh yes, we do!' said Tansy. 'Boys are silly like Teasel. It was his idea!'

'No! Girls are silly like Tansy,' said Teasel. 'It was her idea.'

'I think
they're as silly
as each other,'
laughed Blossom.
'Don't you?'